★

101 Ways to
Read a Book

101

WAYS TO

READ
A BOOK

Timothée de Fombelle

ILLUSTRATED BY
Benjamin Chaud

TRANSLATED BY
Karin Snelson & Angus Yuen-Killick

RED COMET PRESS · BROOKLYN

WARNING

Within these pages you'll find a carefully curated collection of observations . . . specifically, 101 ways to read a book. The illustrations document the varied, and sometimes unpredictable, effects of reading on human beings. However, it should be noted that certain featured poses should only be attempted by adults under the close supervision of a child.

The Sunflower
seeks out the light

The Classic
is surprisingly rare

The Innovator
upends the norm

The Chihuahua becomes tiny
when necessary

The Diva
gives and gives

The Animal Trainer
values teamwork

The Riveted
keeps going until "The End"

The Wildflower
opens in the springtime

The Bookmark

The Lotus

The Bubble

The Ostrich

The Parasol
can bask for hours

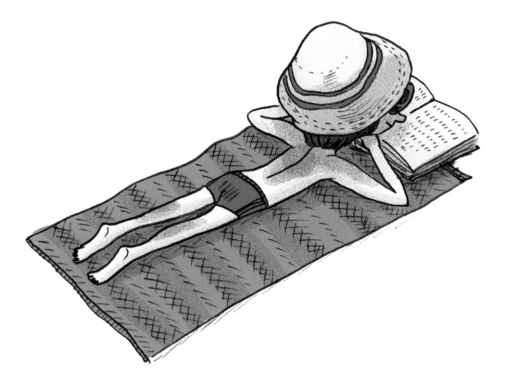

The Lobster
is almost cooked

The Sleepwalker
lives dangerously

The Indestructible
bounces back

The Octopus
doesn't need to choose

The Romantic

can weather any storm

The Champion
takes on the heavyweight

The Wisp
travels light

The Pragmatist
is prepared for any emergency

The Main Course

The Bridge

The Equestrian

The Cowpoke

The Leashed Dog
is trusting

The Sled Dog
prefers long winters

The Snowman

The Drifter

The Eye of the Storm

The Connoisseur
politely declines dessert

The Happy Hermit
stays warm and dry

The Lovebirds
are inseparable

The Ruminants
graze on more than grass

The Goosebump

The Chicken

The Bed Snuggler

The Fireside Cushion Hog

The Passenger
gets carried along

The Storyteller
gets carried away

The Water Lily
is immersed

The Plunderer
ransacks the stacks

The Bedside Rug

The Devoted

The Toboggan

The Mop

The Mop
with chin rest

The Mop
curled up

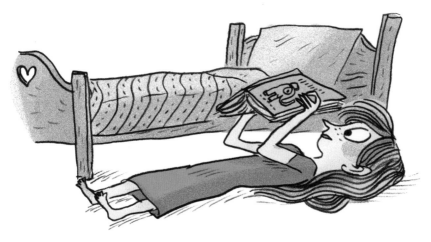

The Mop
supine

The Heap

The Early Bird

The Night Owl

The Snail
is in no hurry

The Ghost
is most active at night

The Explorer
dreams of distant lands

The Co-pilot
is at the ready

The Contortionist

The Cat Up a Tree

The Ripe Fruit

The Inventor

The Thinker

The Dreamer

The Skeptic

The Sentimental

The Snoop
sneaks a peek

The Barbarians
divide and conquer

The Specialist
digs in

The Armchair Acrobat
cannot sit still

The Wiggle Worm
twists and turns

The Spelunker
goes underground

The Burrower
takes temporary cover

The Turtle
is always at home

The Cathedral

The Poseur
sets the scene

The Hipster
plays the part

The Mountain Goat
thrives at high altitude

The Cuddler
loses focus

The Fortress
commands peace

The Sinking Ship
never bails

The Duo The Trio

The Quartet The Anthill

The Pirate
finds buried treasure

The Desert Island
is a world away

The Voracious

The Usurper

The Baggage

The Time-Honored
Tree Leaner

The Free Spirit

The Vine

The Traveler
is indifferent to delays

The Bed Bug
triumphs over adversity

The Heroes
persevere

The Imaginative
transform the world

101 Ways to Read a Book
Text copyright © 2022 Timothée de Fombelle
Illustrations copyright © 2022 Benjamin Chaud

This edition published in 2023 by Red Comet Press LLC, Brooklyn, NY
Translated by Karin Snelson & Angus Yuen-Killick

Original French edition published as *101 façons de lire tout le temps* © 2022 Gallimard Jeunesse

Library of Congress Control Number: 2023930540

ISBN (HB): 978-1-63655-082-4
ISBN (EBOOK): 978-1-63655-083-1

23 24 25 26 27 TLF 10 9 8 7 6 5 4 3 2 1

First Edition
Manufactured in China

RedCometPress.com